# Amelia
## Is Important

# KENNETH BORING

This humble work is dedicated to my amazing wife Gina and my incredible Boring family. They provide inspiration for everything that I do.  And to everyone that embraces their uniqueness as a gift.

Amelia is an airplane.
She lives with her family at the Sunnyville Airport.
Her dad is a big jet that carries people from city to city.
Her mom is a swift helicopter that flies families
over beautiful Lake Sunshine. Her brother is a speedy jet
that zooms across the sky.

Amelia is smart and beautiful.
She is different from the other planes
because she has orange floats instead of wheels.
The other airplanes often make fun of her because
she is different. Her mom and dad always tell her
she is perfect and a very important part of the family.

Amelia always wonders why she is important.
She wishes she were like all the other airplanes.

Amelia's dad, mom, and brother fly every day.
Amelia sits at the airport and watches them
take off and land.
She is sad and wants to help.

Amelia's dad always tips his wing as he leaves the airport.
Amelia knows this is for her.

Amelia's mom hovers over her to make sure she's okay before flying to Lake Sunshine.

Her brother buzzes past the planes
that make fun of her to let them know
he is watching out for his little sister.

Amelia loves her family and she knows they love her,
but she often wonders why she is important.

One afternoon the clouds turned dark
and it begins to storm.
It rains so hard that it floods the airport
and the planes are unable to take off.

The storm causes a big problem.
There is a sick puppy on Sunshine Island
that requires medicine to feel better.

All the airplanes want to help but are unable to take off because of the flooding water.

Amelia`s dad speaks up,

"This is the perfect job for Amelia."

Her floats will allow her to take off in the high water.

She can deliver the medicine to the sick puppy.

Amelia takes off in the high water
and flies through the storm.
She delivers the medicine to Sunshine Island.
The puppy will soon be feeling better.

Amelia receives a hero`s welcoming
as she returns to the airport.

Amelia finally realizes why she is important.
She does not need to be like all the other planes.
She is important because no else can be Amelia.
She is perfect being herself.

# The End

Made in the USA
Lexington, KY
23 July 2019